The Bowerbird

JULIA DONALDSON

CATHERINE RAYNER

MACMILLAN CHILDREN'S BOOKS

A bowerbird, whose name was Bert,
Collected sticks and moss and dirt,
And out of them he built a bower –
A lovely arching twiggy tower.

Said Bert, "That's very good indeed.
And now, a wife is all I need."

He placed a purple flower outside,
Then sat and waited for his bride.

Long hours passed. At last, there came
A female bird, Nanette by name.

"Dear Nanette," the bowerbird said,
"You're just the bird I'd love to wed.
Do you like my purple flower?
Will you come inside my bower?"

Nanette just tossed her haughty head.
"A flower is not enough," she said.

Bert felt hurt, but spread his wings
And flew to find some other things.

Next day, Nanette came back to see
What Bert had laid out lovingly:

A snail shell, a silver bell,
The wrapper from a caramel,
Plus the pretty purple flower.

"Now will you come inside my bower?"

Nanette just tossed her haughty head.
"I don't think much of that," she said.

Bert felt hurt, but hopped away
To find more things for his display.

Next day, Nanette came back and found
Some extra objects on the ground:

A rose hip, a rusty zip,
A pencil and a paperclip,
And then the shell, the silver bell,
The wrapper from the caramel,
Plus the pretty purple flower.

"Now will you come inside my bower?"

Nanette just tossed her haughty head.
"That's still not quite enough," she said.

Bert felt hurt, but off he set
To find yet more for proud Nanette.

When Nanette came by next day
She found a wonderful array:
A fir cone, a stripy stone,
A marble and a mobile phone,

The rose hip, the rusty zip,
The pencil and the paperclip,
The snail shell, the silver bell,
The wrapper from the caramel,
Plus the pretty purple flower.

"*Now* will you come inside my bower?"

Nanette just tossed her haughty head.
"More, more, more!" was all she said.

Bert felt hurt, but off he flew
To search again for treasures new.

He found his choicest items yet,
Then sat and waited for Nanette.

Instead, a bird called Claude came by.
He cocked his head and said, "Nice try –
A pink comb, a garden gnome,
A dented can of shaving foam,
A green pea, a strawberry,
The fairy from a Christmas tree,
A fir cone, a stripy stone,
A marble and a mobile phone,
A rosehip, a rusty zip,
A pencil and a paperclip,

A snail shell, a silver bell,
The wrapper from a caramel,
Plus a rather common flower.
But will she come inside your bower?
I think you're missing just one thing.
How about a golden ring?"

"Thanks," said Bert. "You're very kind,
But that would be quite hard to find."

Said Claude, "I saw one recently,
Hanging from a holly tree.
Turn right, then left – it's very near,
Less than half a mile from here.

Fetch it now! It won't be hard.
Off you go, while I keep guard."

So off went Bert. His heart beat fast.
Nanette would be his bride at last!

Right, past oak and ash he flew,
Then left, past teak and tuckeroo.

Gum trees, tea trees, peach and pine,
Turnipwood and turpentine;

All kinds of trees – but not one holly!
Bert grew tired and melancholy.

No golden ring! The other stuff
Would simply have to be enough.

He turned around and flew back home

But . . .

Where was the comb, the gnome, the foam,
The green pea, the strawberry,
The fairy from the Christmas tree,
The fir cone, the stripy stone,
The marble and the mobile phone,
The rose hip, the rusty zip,
The pencil and the paperclip,
The snail shell, the silver bell,
The wrapper from the caramel?

Where was the thief? He searched around,
Until he heard a squawking sound
And there, outside another bower,
Were all his things (except the flower).
Inside the bower sat Claude. Worse yet . . .

. . . Sitting beside him was Nanette.

Bert went home. He sat and sighed.
"Perhaps I'll never find a bride.
I'm giving up!" But then he heard
The footsteps of another bird . . .

The sweetest bird he'd ever seen.
She bowed her head and said, "I'm Jean."

She looked Bert over once or twice
And added, "You look very nice,
And what a pretty purple flower!"
And then . . .

. . . she came inside his bower.

For
Sara and Robin Bowers
JD

For
Beatrice Bird
CR

© Steve Ullathorne

JULIA DONALDSON has written some of the world's best-loved children's books, including *The Gruffalo* and *What the Ladybird Heard*. She was Children's Laureate 2011-13 and has a CBE for Services to Literature. Julia and her husband Malcolm divide their time between West Sussex and Edinburgh, and love wildlife. Julia was inspired to write *The Bowerbird* after watching an episode of the BBC series 'Natural World', in which David Attenborough talked about the birds' amazing behaviour.

© Blue Sky Photography

CATHERINE RAYNER is an award-winning author and illustrator. She studied Illustration at Edinburgh College of Art, and still lives in the city with her husband and two sons. In 2009 Catherine won the prestigious CILIP Kate Greenaway Medal. Catherine loves animals and has a horse, a cat, a dog, a hamster, a goldfish and two water snails which all inspire her work but, so far, no birds.

© featherollector/iStock

THE BOWERBIRD is a real bird that lives in Australia and Papua New Guinea. Bowerbirds are famous for their courting behaviour, where male birds build a 'bower' to attract a female and collect objects with which to decorate it. Male bowerbirds will spend hours arranging their impressive collection. However, some sneaky bowerbirds will steal decorations from other birds for their own bower!

First published 2023 by Macmillan Children's Books
an imprint of Pan Macmillan
The Smithson, 6 Briset Street, London, EC1M 5NR
EU representative: Macmillan Publishers Ireland Limited, 1st Floor, The Liffey Trust Centre,
117-126 Sheriff Street Upper, Dublin 1, D01 YC43
Associated companies throughout the world
www.panmacmillan.com

ISBN 978-1-5290-9224-0

MIX
Paper | Supporting responsible forestry
FSC® C116313
FSC
www.fsc.org